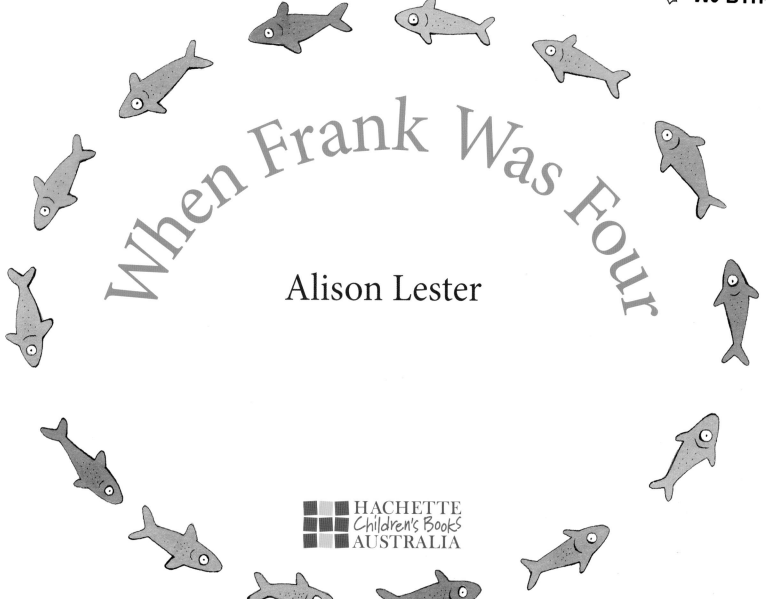

When Frank Was Four

Alison Lester

HACHETTE
Children's Books
AUSTRALIA

One

When Nicky was one she tipped spaghetti on her head.

Frank bit the dog.

Tessa took her first step

Celeste ate the cat food.　　Ernie bashed the saucepans.　　And Rosie said 'Horse'.

But Clive smashed the china
at his Great Grandmother's birthday party.

Two

When Frank was two he loved to wave goodnight to the moon.

A kangaroo stole Rosie's chips.

Tessa stopped wearing nappies.

Ernie climbed into the fish tank.

Celeste began to sleep all night.

And once at the supermarket, Clive just couldn't wait.

But Nicky got lost on Christmas Eve.

 # Three

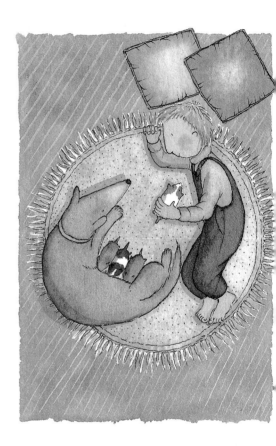

When Clive was three he danced in his cousin's tutu.

Ernie gave away his dummy.

Frank's dog had puppies.

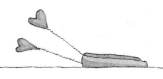
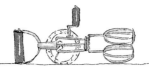

Rosie began to play the guitar.

Celeste was given a chicken for her birthday.

And Nicky got stuck up a tree.

But Tessa made a pudding.

Four

When Frank was four he ate three packets of fruity fish.

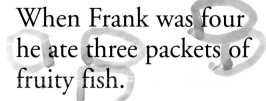

Nicky cut off her plait.

Tessa dressed up the cat.

Ernie started to wear glasses.

Clive took off his training wheels.

And Rosie's pony arrived on Christmas morning.

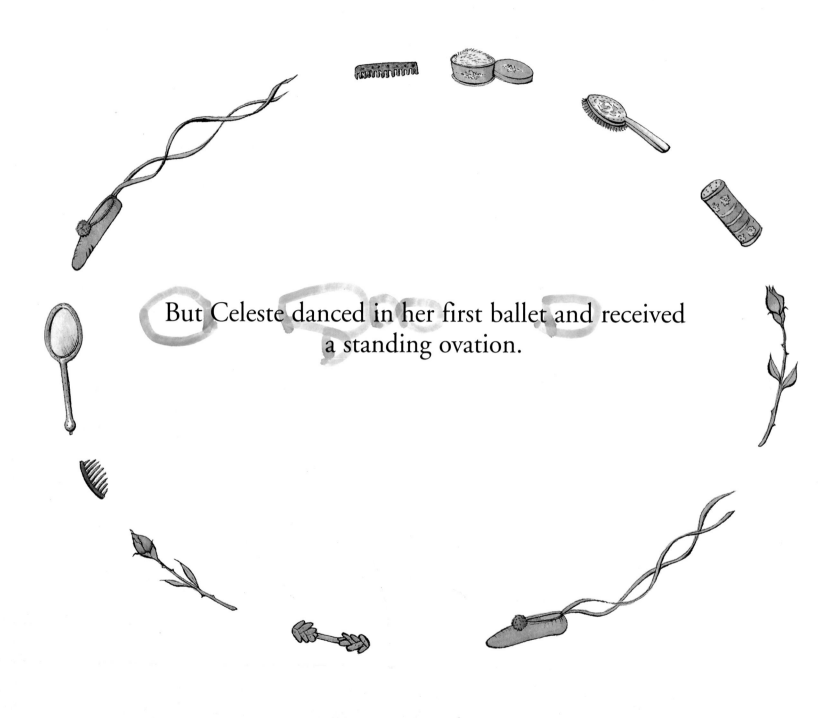

But Celeste danced in her first ballet and received
a standing ovation.

Five

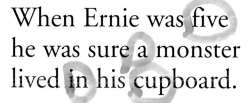

When Ernie was five
he was sure a monster
lived in his cupboard.

Celeste made a
snowman.

Rosie got a baby sister.

Nicky broke her arm.

Clive's mother sewed his alligator doona.

And Tessa swam right across the pool.

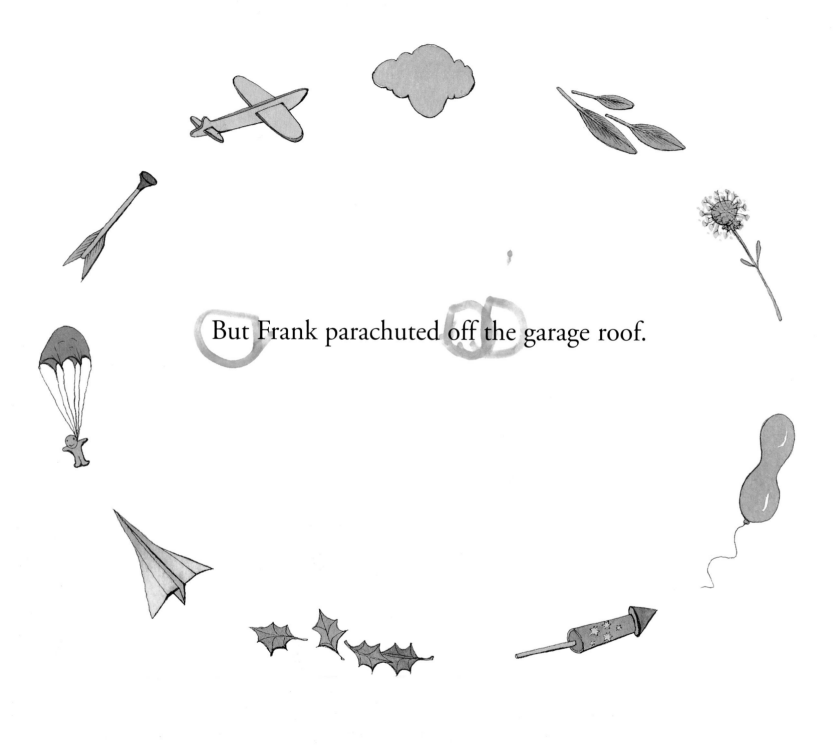

But Frank parachuted off the garage roof.

Six

When Nicky was six she did a somersault on the trampoline.

Frank kidnapped his Grandmother's cat.

Ernie's lizard had babies.

Clive made a crocodile-shaped birthday cake.

Tessa ran away from home.

And Celeste wore her pyjama pants to school.

Seven

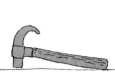 

When Celeste was seven she had her first filling.

Nicky flew off the swing.

Rosie climbed Uluru.

Frank built a spaceship.

And Tessa gave Clive his first kiss.

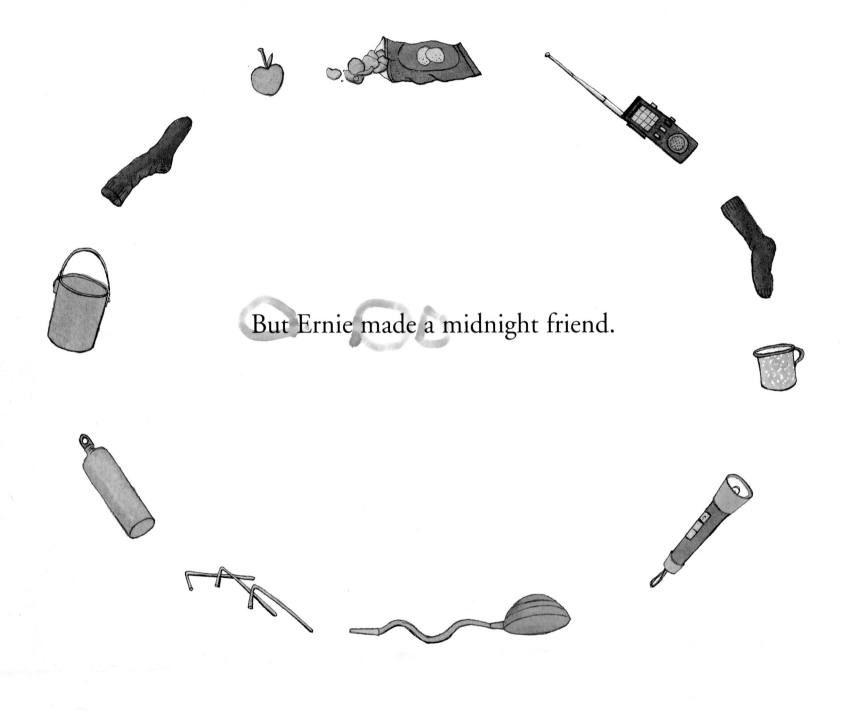

But Ernie made a midnight friend.

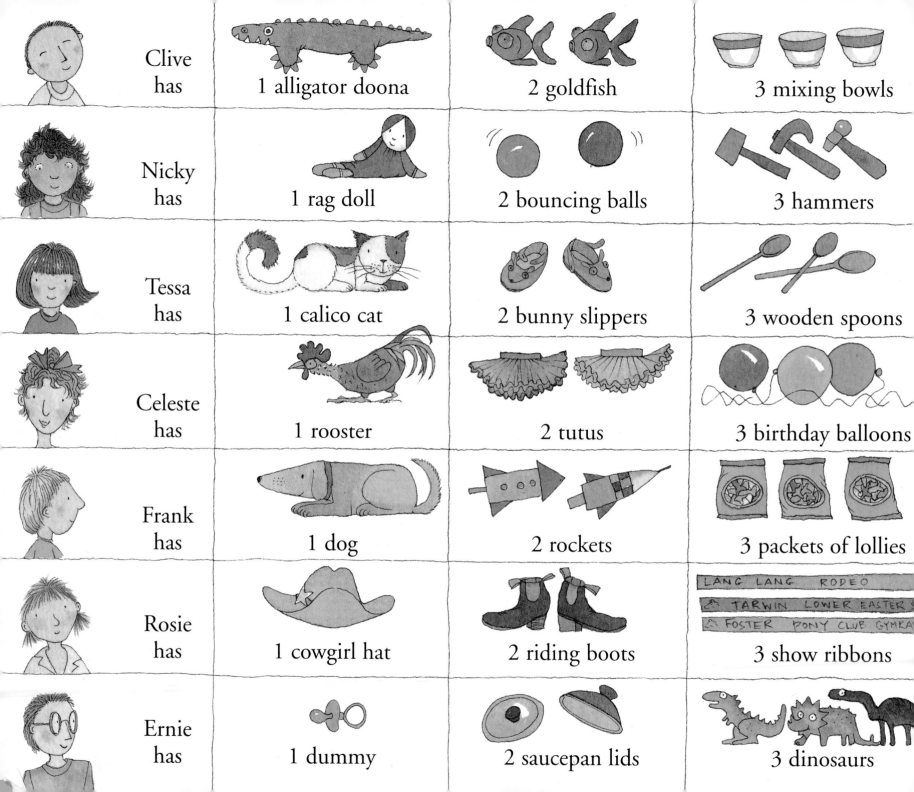

Clive has	1 alligator doona	2 goldfish	3 mixing bowls
Nicky has	1 rag doll	2 bouncing balls	3 hammers
Tessa has	1 calico cat	2 bunny slippers	3 wooden spoons
Celeste has	1 rooster	2 tutus	3 birthday balloons
Frank has	1 dog	2 rockets	3 packets of lollies
Rosie has	1 cowgirl hat	2 riding boots	3 show ribbons
Ernie has	1 dummy	2 saucepan lids	3 dinosaurs

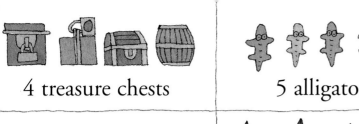

4 treasure chests

5 alligator pops

6 toffee apples

7 coloured pencils

4 bananas

5 autumn leaves

6 socks

7 screws

4 tea cups

5 sandcastles

6 tails

7 snakes

4 feathers

5 ballet shoes

6 special soaps

7 bottles of perfume

4 puppies

5 karate books

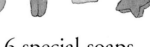

6 chocolate biscuits

7 favourite stars

4 horseshoes

5 lime spiders

6 tadpoles

7 lollypops

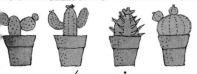

4 cacti

5 baby lizards

6 strawberries

7 tentpegs

For Helen and Woofa

This edition published in Australia and New Zealand in 2006
by Hachette Children's Books Australia
(an imprint of Hachette Livre Australia Pty Ltd)
Level 17, 207 Kent Street, Sydney NSW 2000
Website: www.hachette.com.au

First published by Hodder Headline Australia in 1994
Published in paperback 1995
Reprinted in 1995, 1997, 1998, 2000 (twice), 2001, 2008

National Library of Australia Cataloguing-in-Publication data

Lester, Alison.
When Frank was four.

ISBN 978 0 7336 2108 6.
I. Title.
A823.3

Printed in China